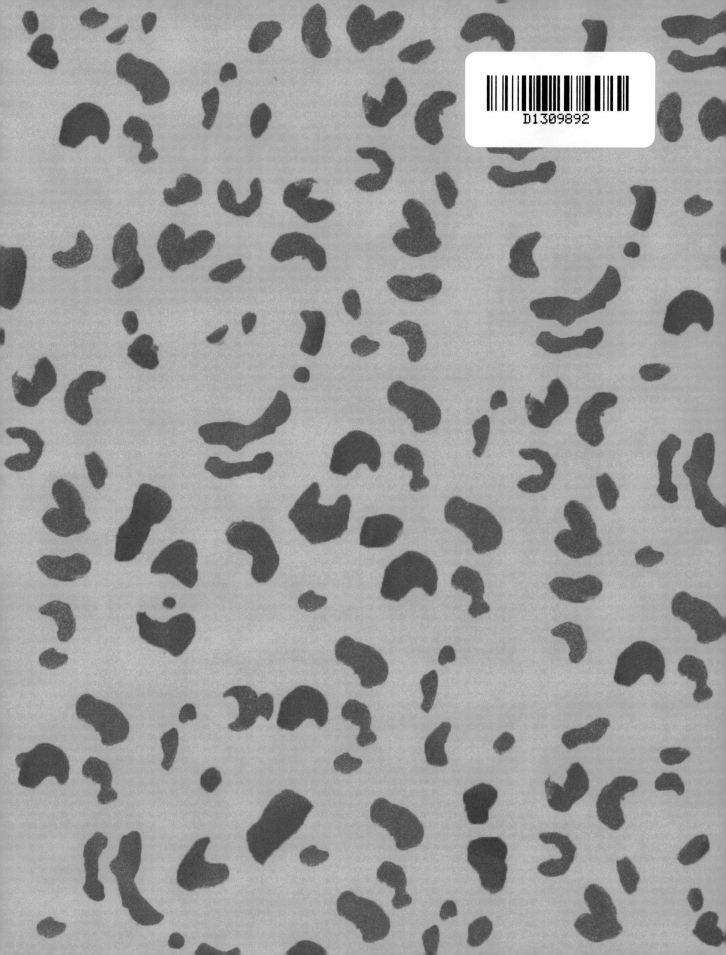

THE TEN LEOPARDS

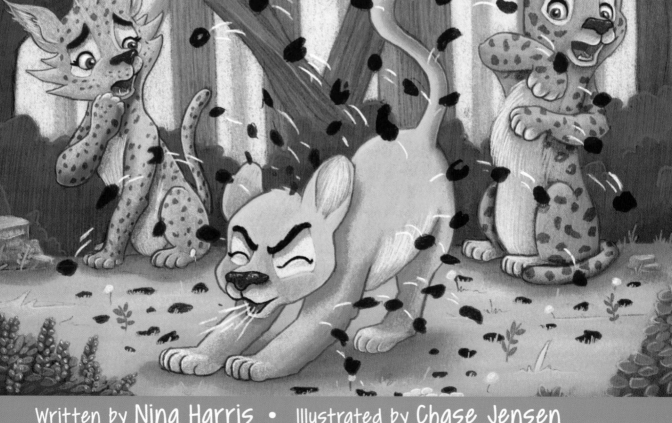

Written by **Nina Harris** • Illustrated by **Chase Jensen**

CFI • An imprint of Cedar Fort, Inc. • Springville, Utah

To my son, Edward
–Nina

Text © 2019 Nina Harris
Illustrations © 2019 Chase Jensen
All rights reserved.

ISBN 13: 978-1-4621-3587-5

Published by CFI, an imprint of Cedar Fort, Inc.
2373 W. 700 S., Springville, UT 84663
Distributed by Cedar Fort, Inc., www.cedarfort.com

Library of Congress Control Number: 2019932868

Cover design and typesetting by Shawnda T. Craig
Cover design © 2019 Cedar Fort, Inc.
Edited by Kaitlin Barwick

Printed in the United States of America

10 9 8 7 6 5 4 3 2 1

Printed on acid-free paper

Pouncer the leopard had many friends,
Like Whiskers, and Tickles, and Claws.

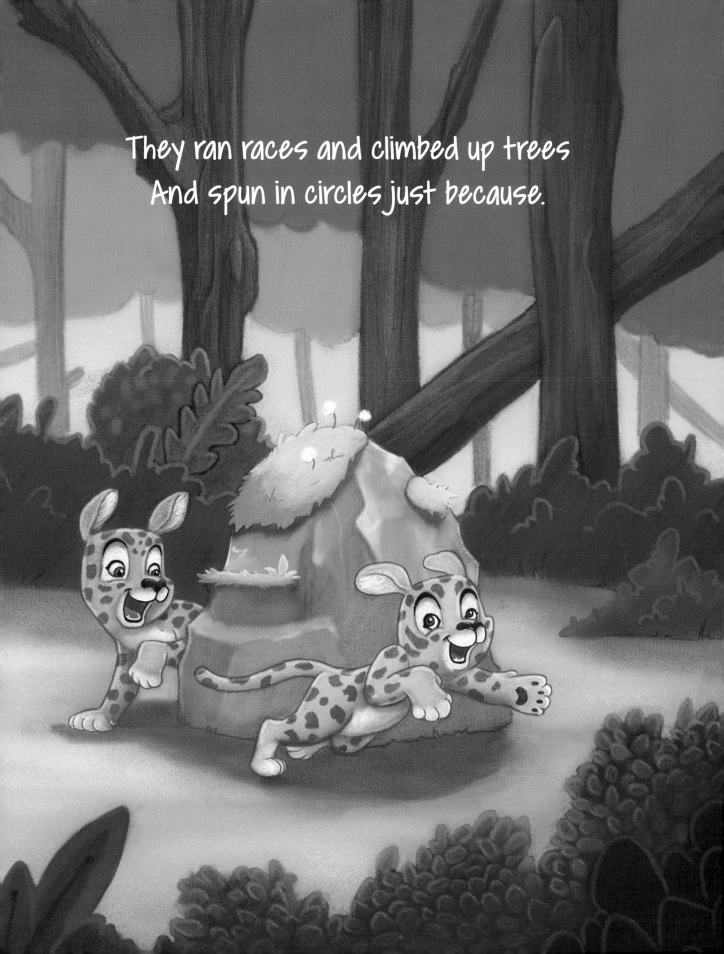

They ran races and climbed up trees
And spun in circles just because.

All the leopards loved these games,
But the thing they loved the most

Was sitting in the sun and showing off
Their beautiful spotted coats.

One day, Pouncer looked around
And found some friends were gone.
So he went out to check
If something was wrong.

He found Whiskers huddled in a cave
Feeling very cold.

Tickles was hiding in some leaves.
He wouldn't come out, we're told.

Pouncer knew things were bad
When he saw Claws had caught a cough.

He sniffled and he sneezed,
And then his spots fell off!

All the leopards were alarmed
And backed far away.
"What is a leopard without his spots?"
They thought with dismay.

It wasn't long before Pouncer, too,
Was sick with all his friends.
And when they counted all of them,
They found they numbered ten.

Now there was a great Healer,
Who lived up on the mountain.
They decided to go to him
To see if he could help them.

Sniffling, sneezing, and wheezing,
They climbed into the hills.
And when they found the Healer,
They called, "Please help! We're very ill."

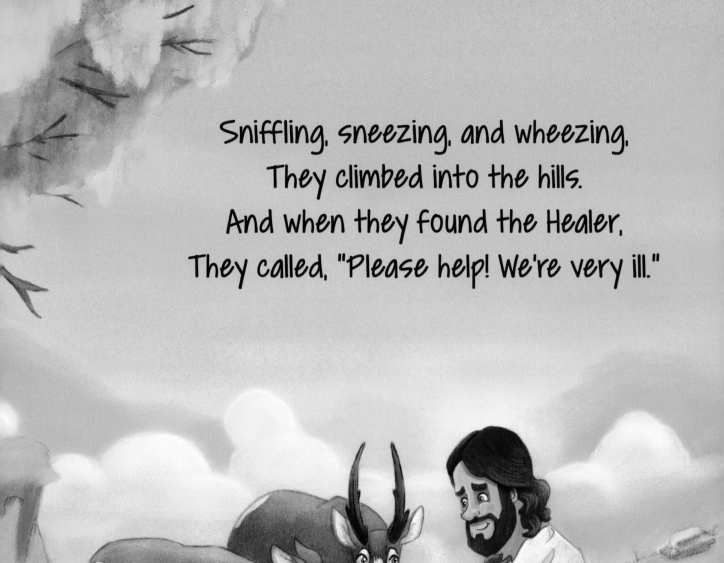

The Healer came at once
And touched each weary head.

"My name is Jesus, and you'll be fine.
Now get some sleep," he said.

And when the sun came up,
They awoke all polka-dotted.

They pounced and played and climbed up trees.
"We feel great!" they shouted.

Pouncer saw Jesus,
And he dashed to his side.
Smiling, he licked him.
"Thank You! Thank You!" he cried.

"I'm always glad to help," Jesus said.
"But weren't there ten of you?"
Pouncer turned to call his friends,
But they were racing out of view.

Pouncer was sad his friends were gone.
But he decided to stay.

He truly loved Jesus
And helped him every day.

Pouncer learned that Jesus
Loves each and every one,
And he will help all of us
If we will just come.

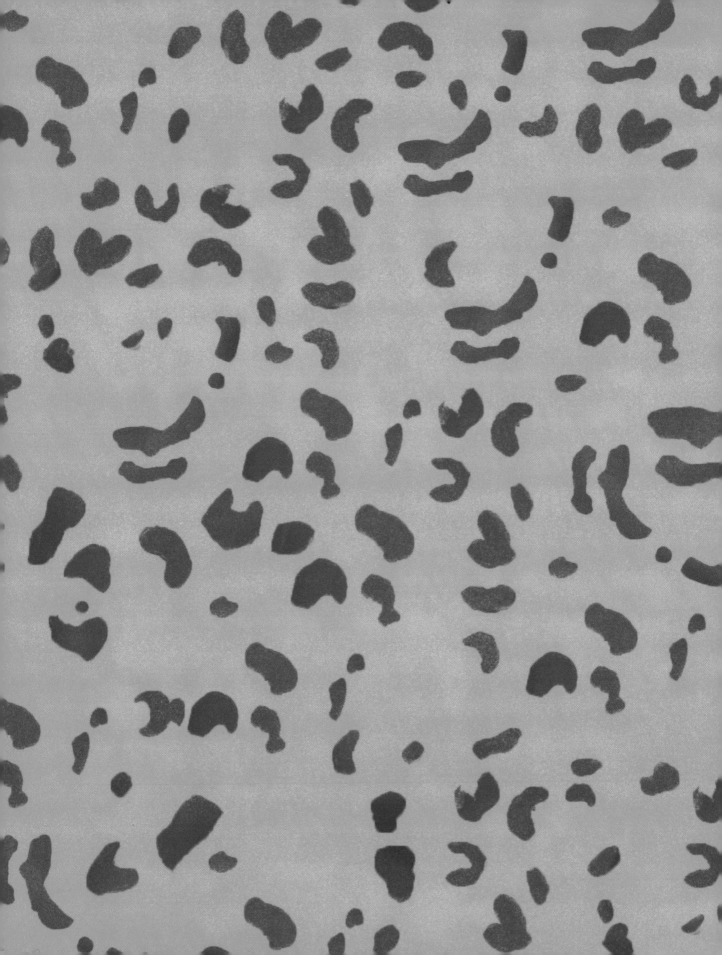